ROSES

What is fairer than a rose?
What is sweeter?

George Herbert (1593–1633)

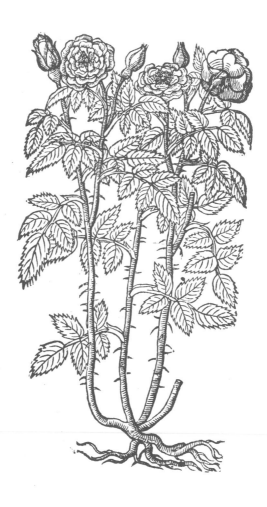

ROSES

Orietta Sala

With illustrations by the author

MICHAEL JOSEPH

First published in Great Britain in 1989 by
Webb & Bower (Publishers) Limited,
9 Colleton Crescent, Exeter, Devon EX2 4BY,
in association with Michael Joseph Limited,
27 Wright's Lane, London W8 5TZ

Penguin Books Ltd, Registered Offices: Harmondsworth,
Middlesex, England
Penguin Books Australia Ltd, Ringwood, Victoria, Australia
Penguin Books Canada Ltd, 2801 John Street, Markham, Ontario,
Canada L3R 1D4
Penguin Books (NZ) Ltd, 182–190 Wairau Road, Auckland 10, New Zealand

Designed by Carlotta Maderna / Katia Marassi / Vic Giolitto
Series Editor Mariarosa Schiaffino
With illustrations by Orietta Sala

Production by Nick Facer / Rob Kendrew

Translated from the Italian by Kerry Milis
Copyright © 1988 Idealibri SpA, Milan
Copyright © 1989 Idealibri SpA, Milan, for English translation

British Library Cataloguing in Publication Data

Orietta Sala
Roses.
1. Roses
I. Title II. Series III. Le mie rose *English*
583′.372
ISBN 0–86350–303–9

Typeset in Great Britain by Scribes, Exeter, Devon

Printed and bound in Italy by Vallardi Industrie Grafiche

CONTENTS

PREFACE

A PERSON with clear ideas and defined tastes, Orietta does not like half measures. It is difficult to give her a present, impossible to give her ordinary flowers. Heaven knows how her suitors – she must have had flocks of them in the past and still has several – when they come courting her with flowers dare risk her displeasure by presenting her with an ostentatious bouquet or – worse – offering her a hastily chosen plant or a pre-wrapped bunch from the florist's.

'My roses? Of course they are not the usual kinds. Would you expect me to be satisfied with Baccarat, so stiff, so rigid? Why should I deprive myself of the languid foliage of an old-fashioned rose, like the Complicata – which is not at all complicated to grow – with its big, beautiful, brilliant-pink flowers fading to white in the centre? Why should I be satisfied with a rose that can be found in any nursery when there are others for my garden that are more unusual, that give me more genuine happiness, that are more . . . me?'

These are questions that need only one answer: this book. Because if it is true that Orietta is a woman who lives, loves and breathes flowers with all her soul and expresses her feelings in her paintings, it is also true that there are more and more among us – finally! – who are also passionate about these flowers, which unite a joyful spirit and a love for gardening like no other.

Cultivating a small plot of land to make it beautiful, decorative and satisfying means growing roses, or at least it should include them. You will get incomparable gifts from your land without very much difficulty ('roses will come, they always come!'); incredible shades of colour; a sense of the fragility of the life that trembles on the stem, in an unexpected and emotional flowering, in soft perfume, or the wonder of a shiny insect on a blossom.

Growing roses is all this and more, especially if you want to choose the perfect rose for an occasion, to create an atmosphere and please personal tastes, perhaps a rose that is unusual, one that has been around for many years but has been overlooked recently. Such roses, flowers of old-fashioned simplicity, and incomparable for their grace and style, have finally recovered from the oblivion to which they were confined by obsessive experimentation and continuous hybridization.

These old roses are not the only protagonists of this book, but they certainly dominate it. Slight and diaphanous, or showy and vibrant, with full petals curled up scroll-like or closed like a flute, sometimes with mossy sepals, sometimes with golden stamens, with petals arranged singly or, sharp and jagged, in clusters, with scented blossoms weighing down their branches or the blooms standing proudly on their stems with aristocratic bearing, the foliage blue-green and shiny or soft and woolly, full of sharp thorns or sparsely covered – the possibilities are endless and enchanting and you can become so caught up in the subject that, as one rose enthusiast who wrote a book called *Extravagant Botany* said, you 'shiver with delight'.

Some roses are more suited to showy flowerbeds in full view, while others find their ideal spot in some quiet corner. Some like to send out long meandering shoots, creeping along over everything as they go; others grow into tidy compact bushes or impenetrable hedges with a tangle of thorny branches. There are some that are so adaptable that they can grow on sand and others that need support, happily embracing a tree or a column.

Old roses, neither arrogant nor aloof, capable of infinite and diverse beauty, call to mind the poets, like the Greek Anacreon:

> The rose is the perfume of the Gods,
> The joy of men,
> It adorns the blossoming charms of Love,
> It is Venus's dearest flower.

There is only one risk in pursuing old roses, and that is that all the other more modern ones will seem less attractive, even false.

MARIAROSA SCHIAFFINO

INTRODUCTION

NO flower in the world has been more beloved, more cultivated, more often mentioned than the rose. Such tribute
is fully merited by this queen of flowers.

But the rose is also the flower that has been the most
manipulated by people, so much that we may wonder if most
of the roses we have in our gardens are not the results of
laboratory experiments. A rose that is classified as a 'Modern'
rose has genes from thirty or forty different roses and is the
result of years of patience and infinite efforts at hybridization.

This thought is somewhat disturbing. Also disturbing is the
hint of madness behind so much fanaticism, in the ambition
to squeeze out of such a beautiful, sweet and pure thing, something so modest as heart, everything, from the possible to the
impossible.

Do we demand of any other flower that it bloom all year
round? That its blossoms grow ever larger? And if it is red or
white, that it become black or blue? Yet we ask all kinds of
things of the rose: to bloom longer, to last eternally, to come
in all colours. We want it to resist cold and heat, to resist
disease, to resist the wind, not to be damaged by the rain. We
almost seem to want a plastic flower, though in the best sense
of the word. Yes, today's roses are perfect flowers; and when
we admire their triumphant and dazzling blossoms open in
the May sun, they are incomparable.

But once you begin to grow roses and, finding yourself
driven to know more and possess more, let yourself be swept
up by a true passion for them (and it is so easy to be thus
carried away), you cannot stop there. Inevitably you must go
back again over the course of history to find out about the
origins of the rose. When you discover that in the past other
roses were the favourites, in all likelihood you will want to
see if those roses were worthier of love than today's roses.
Sacheverell Sitwell once wrote, in a book on the subject, that
it was enough to order some roses like Stanwell Perpetual and
Mme Pierre Oger and wait for summer, for no one who had
even a modest collection of these Old roses would feel any
more interest in Modern roses.

And at last we reach the motive behind my long discourse:
roses created in the past century and even earlier, discovered
by chance by an *aficionado* or a professional gardener, botanical specimens and their hybrids, are coming back into our

gardens. These roses are still being taught to flower year round or to have superb full blossoms, without using up everything they have. But their nature is different. It is all poetry and delicacy, fragility and perishability, even simplicity and humility. A small trembling flower, with a short life, does not produce less intense emotions than a pompous flower with showy beauty. The contrary is probably true.

The rose however remains an immortal flower. Neither people nor time nor fashion nor whim can make it disappear. Its charm will last forever.

What is the reason for such beauty? The rose keeps the secret of its mysterious fascination to itself; it remains silent and is loved.

And truly the rose has always been loved. It has accompanied human beings and their history throughout civilization. It has even gone before them. In the Baltic basin, rose fossils have been found going back 20 million years. They are preserved in the Museum of Roses in Hay-les-Roses, near Paris. Other prehistoric roses have been found in the United States in Oregon and Colorado, and in India, as testimony to the widespread growth of the flower.

Coming down through the centuries to our own age, we find the first written documents. Here there are many references to the rose: every culture, every group of people mentions them.

King Sargon in the third millennium before Christ, re-entered the city of Ur from a military expedition bringing with him 'vines, figs and roses', the Egyptians put roses in the tombs of their pharaohs to accompany them on their voyage to the afterlife. Confucius tells of the emperor Chin Nun in 2690BC who was passionate about roses and Confucius himself owned more than 600 volumes on the cultivation of this flower. The rose triumphed in Greek civilization too: Achilles's shield was adorned with roses; Anacreon tells the beautiful legend of the white rose which, along with Venus, was born from the foam of the sea.

A symbol of pleasure and of pain – the blossom gives pleasure, the thorns give pain – it is not surprising that the rose became the flower of love, sacred to Venus. In every ancient civilization it took on this symbolic value. Later, in Christian mythology, it became a symbol of pure love, of the Virgin Mary, the Mystical Rose, the rose without thorns.

Thus the rose, coming from the foam of the sea, was born white, as Botticelli's famous painting shows us. But another legend shows how it quickly turned red. Venus, running to help the wounded Adonis, pricked her foot on a rose thorn and the blood of the goddess coloured the flowers vermilion.

Love, and the colours pink and red, have always been connected. Such a marriage is encouraged by the poets, and in texts the rose, whose very name is a colour, is portrayed mostly as red, vermilion or purple: vermilion for Petrarch, red for Chaucer, purple for Ariosto. Red too for Robert Burns, whose love is 'like a red, red rose'.

The other quality which makes a rose a rose is its fragility. Love is as brief as a rose, life is as brief as a rose. Ronsard's famous rose in his sonnet *'Mignonne allons voir si la rose'* lasted only *'du matin au soir'* and Clement Marot's rose is the symbol of a tender young girl kidnapped from death: *'Rose elle a vécu ce que vivent les roses, l'espace d'un matin'*. However, the poet bitterly adds, *'Elle était du monde où les plus belles choses ont le pire destin'*. 'Gather ye rosebuds while ye may', counsels Robert Herrick, nor must one forget the rose of the Persian poet of *The Rubaiyat*, since the rose is so much at home in Persia. The theme is always more or less the same and it is always melancholic. 'What is a rose? One thing is certain, life is fleeting, the rest is lies. The rose only flowers once and then it dies forever.'

As for references to the complexion and especially to the cheek, one could write volumes. Cheeks are always as velvety as a peach and as red as a rose. *'Zéphire est de merveille et d'amour atteint, voyant des roses sur son teint'*, sings Théophile de Viaux. For Foscolo, the rose is languid.

Convention has it that the rose is always accompanied by the violet. Sappho started it with 'I do not know if you will forget, and you forget, our celestial suffering, the sweet garlands of roses and violets . . .' For Sappho the garlands were actually intertwined, while other poets only seemed to know of these flowers because they had read about them somewhere. Otherwise why would they not have tried to combine other flowers? For Carducci, it was 'the smell of roses and violets', for Leopardi 'a posy of roses and violets'. At least Rabindranath Tagore mentions 'jasmine and roses, violets and chrysanthemums'.

Pascoli is very distracted; even though he is from the country, for him roses are only creepers. It is rather interesting to follow the thoughts of poets and writers through the infinite transformations of the rose, and realize that it was like a precious magic potion that could be refilled with a thousand different perfumes.

William Blake said: 'O Rose, thou art sick'; For Mallarmé the rose became 'cruel': *'Pareille à la chair de la femme, la rose est cruelle'*. Swinburne would gladly have changed 'the lily of virtue for the rose of vice'. Apollinaire's rose was 'ardent', Stigliani's was 'delicate'. For Marinetti, the Futurist poet, the rose was 'diabolic' and in his crazy cookery he advises us to eat it. T S Eliot called it 'scorched'. And in 'Ash Wednesday', we have a whole series of epithets: 'exhausted', 'life-giving', 'worried', 'reposeful'. The rose in effect represents everything. 'Inviolate' for Thomas Hardy, for Emily Dickinson, the roses in autumn are 'out of town'. Govoni defined it 'the pale unconscious rose', and Gozzano saw it as a flame, 'guiding the bicycle, lit up with a huge bouquet of roses, in its ascent'. In D'Annunzio's rose gardens roses were 'extenuating' while for Rilke the rose is, in the title of one of his poems, 'pure incoherence'. Neruda saw in the rose, the colour of the cheek and the secret beauty of the belly: 'fresh arms of flowers and a belly of rose'. But perhaps the most lovely homage to the rose was made, again by Neruda, when he writes, '*pequeña rosa, rosa pequeña*'.

A Brief History

THERE is no agreement on the number of species of wild roses; it ranges from 100 to 150. The species grows in the northern hemisphere, particularly in the temperate zones, from eastern Asia – where 85 per cent of them grow – through Russia and Turkey, across all of Europe except Iceland, to North America.

As we have seen, the rose was mentioned very early in history, but references in ancient texts are vague regarding names and types. According to testimony from Herodotus, we know that it could have five or sixty petals and that it grew in the garden of King Midas. Pliny mentions roses cultivated in Paestum. Not only were they grown in private gardens but they were the subject of extensive cultivation once it was learned how to extract their essence from the fragrant blossoms. In the vast Roman Empire some fifty species were known and cultivated. Those found growing naturally in Italy today are the *sempervirens, arvensis, pendulina, canina, pimpinellifolia, gallica, rubrifolia* and *eglanteria.*

Species roses which have played an important role in the creation of the roses cultivated in gardens today are the following.

Rosa gallica

A large compact shrub with few thorns, and full foliage, it is a genuine species and perhaps the oldest of its kind. This is probably the Middle Eastern and Persian sacred rose and the one cultivated by the Greeks and later the Romans. From the *gallica,* came, through spontaneous cross-pollination, other roses like the *alba,* the *damascena* and the *centifolia.* It assumed great importance during the Middle Ages both for medicinal reasons and for the production of its essence. The Apothecary's Rose is in fact *Rosa gallica officinalis.* It also was equally important in heraldry, becoming a symbol fo the royal house of Lancaster and a symbol of Christianity. At the beginning of the nineteenth century it was grown in the gardens of Malmaison by Empress Josephine, who knew 200 different varieties. Among the most famous and the oldest known are the *Rosa gallica versicolor* or *Rosa mundi,* with variegated petals, and the Complicata.

Rosa x damascena

Its origin is not known but it is certainly not a species though it may be a natural hybrid, even a result of several hybrids, based on the *gallica*. Certainly it was grown in the classical world and it is mentioned by Pliny. It has a double corolla, grey-green leaves, thorny stem and very fragrant flowers. It was considered the most fragrant rose and also the most often cultivated for the extraction of its scent. There are two types of *damascena*, the summer *damascena* (from which we derive the *alba*) and the autumn *damascena*, important because it passed on to its hybrids a second, later-flowering season. Among those cultivated the most famous are Celsiana, Ispahan and Mme Hardy.

Rosa x alba

This was probably familiar to the ancient world and certainly to people in the Middle Ages. With beautiful leafy sepals and grey-green foliage, this rose is also originally a hybrid, probably the result of a natural cross between a *damascena*, a *canina* and a *gallica*. It is robust and generally free from diseases; the weight of its heavy corolla with its semi-double petals often causes the branches to droop. It was perhaps the white rose

which gave England its old name, Albion, and it is the emblem of the house of York. Precise references to this rose can be found after the sixteenth century when Turner, the father of English botany, describes the most popular forms: the *semiplena*, with a lovely scent and perfect shape, and Maiden's Blush.

Rosa moschata

Originally from the Himalayas and grown in India, it was naturalized in the ancient world of the Mediterranean. A rose which does not like frost, it is characterized by clusters of white flowers, a musky scent and thick foliage. It is one of the flowers most often grown commercially, for its scent.

Rosa x centifolia

Of unknown origin, it is probably a complicated natural hybrid in which the *gallica* and the *canina* crossed through the *Rosa alba*. We do not know if it was grown by the ancients; our records only begin in the sixteenth century when it was in the possession of the Dutch who through arduous work created new varieties from it. The French obtained other varieties and began to cultivate this rose in Provence. Many *centifolia* hybrids have French names: Fantin-Latour, Reine des Centfeuilles and Rose des Meaux, a dwarf shrub with small flowers. *Rosa x centifolia* is an opulent rose that often has a

languid appearance because the weight of the flowers pulls the stems over.

Rosa x centifolia muscosa

This is a natural genetic mutation from *Rosa centifolia* and it is characterized by calyx and stalk covered with a thick down that resembles moss and resin-scented glands on the sepals. Famous varieties are Mousseline, Blanche Moreau, General Kleber, and Gloire des Mousseux.

Rosa chinensis

The introduction in Europe through merchants and navigators of roses from China marks an important change in the history of the rose. In the course of the seventeenth century, the first though not the most important arrived, namely the *bracteata* and the *banksiae*.

The beginning of the great production of garden roses, came in the nineteenth century from four roses, not species but hybrids of roses like the *chinensis*, the *gigantea* and the *odorata* (probably a cross between the other two), which are known today as the founding mothers: the Parker's Pink China, Slater's Crimson China and, a little later, Hume's Blush China and Park's Yellow China, the last with a tea-like scent.

From the Nineteenth-century Rose to the Rose of Today

With the arrival of the Chinese rose, and thanks to the indefatigable work of growers and hybridists, the golden age of roses began. A huge number of varieties was created, and these were then classified in more or less homogeneous groupings.

Bourbon rose

The first were natural hybrids from Bourbon (the island now called Reunion), a cross between an autumn-flowering *Rosa damascena* and a *Rosa chinensis*, Pink China. Over this base French hybridists created many plants that are still treasured today such as Souvenir de la Malmaison, Mme Pierre Oger, Reine Victoria, Bourbon Queen and Zéphirine Drouhin which is thornless. Shrubs or excellent climbers, valued for their continuity of bloom, their colour shading, their exquisite scent (which comes from the *damascena*), some varieties have become veritable antiques today but their fascination is still indisputable.

Rosa x noisettiana

Developed by Philippe Noisette in America and then sent to France, it was born of a cross between a Pink China and a *Rosa moschata*. The first variety, still grown today, was the Blush Noisette. Others that are popular are Aimée Vibert, Céline Forestier and Maréchal Niel. Generally speaking, they are vigorous climbers.

Perpetual rose

At the end of the eighteenth century a rose flourished in France (probably the result of a cross between an autumn-flowering *damascena*, a *gallica* and a China) that was loved for its long flowering season. When it went to England it was rebaptized the Duchess of Portland. From it descended the Rose du Roi which, crossed with a China rose, became the founder of a whole group of roses with large blossoms and a longer flowering season. It was called the Hybrid Perpetual and some of its star varieties are the Reine des Violettes, Paul Neyron and Frau Karl Druschki.

Tea rose

This is not a homogeneous easily classifiable group. A climbing rose with a tea-like scent, it does not tolerate cold well. It was created by crosses first in the East and later in Europe betwen Hume's Blush China and Park's Yellow China. Its antecedents were in the *Rosa chinensis* and the *Rosa odorata* and their varieties. It dominated the stage along with the Perpetual rose until the middle of the nineteenth century.

Hybrid Tea rose

The aim of nursery people at this point was to combine the elegance, variety of colours and scents of the Tea rose with the resistance to cold and disease of the Perpetual rose. After various genetic problems and a long period of experimentation crossing various roses, a very important new variety was developed, the Hybrid Tea, destined to supplant almost all other garden roses. Thanks to studies made by Pernet, hybrid yellows were also added. The Hybrid Teas are generally bedding and cutting roses, flourishing plants with large flowers. They are the roses that are usually most familiar to people when talking about roses.

Polyantha, Polyantha hybrid and Floribunda roses

Another rose coming from the East, the Japanese *Rosa multiflora* or *polyantha*, also played its part in the evolution of the flower. The Frenchman Guillot, working with this rose and other China hybrids, obtained the Polyantha roses, which are no longer grown today. They served as a base for the Dane Poulsen and later the Englishman LeGrice to obtain new and successful crosses of the Polyantha hybrid, rebaptized the Floribunda. It is a very popular group, botanically speaking, which is not very homogeneous, containing hardy shrubs with flowering clusters. One of the characteristics of this group is a long and repeated flowering season, wide variety and the ability to create strong colour effects. Generally they are not strongly scented. Some stars are Escapade and Iceberg which are scented, and City of Leeds, Sarabande, and Yesterday.

Modern rose

The Hybrid Tea roses, classified as shrub and bedding roses in catalogues, the Floribunda rose, called bouquet roses, and many other roses whose complicated origins do not permit their inclusion in any recognizable group, make up what is commonly called the Modern rose. In the last category are rambling roses.

Miniature rose

These come from a China rose, *Rosa chinensis minima* also called *Rosa roulettii* because the first of these roses to be born in Europe chose for the occasion the balcony of one Dr Roulet, in Switzerland. They are very small roses with perfectly shaped but miniature blossoms. In recent times, Spain and the United States have focused on these cutting roses which today enjoy a certain popularity.

THE DIFFERENT TYPES
AND THEIR CARE

WHETHER for their botanical characteristics or for their destination in the garden, roses can be divided into two separate categories: shrub roses, approximately 2½–6 feet (¾– 2 metres) tall, and tall roses. There are actually three varieties of tall roses, the rambler, the pillar rose, and the so-called climber, though that is not a completely appropriate term for it since it has no tendrils or suckers with which to attach itself.

The pillar roses are not terribly vigorous but they have shoots that reach up to 6–9 feet (2–3 metres) long which allows them to be trained around a support such as a column or pillar or pole or even a tree. They can also be trained around a gate or an arch so they can show off the beauty of their romantic and picturesque flowers.

The climber on the other hand puts out shoots that develop into strong, hardy branches many feet, several metres, high. It generally has large single flowers, with two flowering seasons, and requires pruning.

The rambler, a fair number of which come from *Rosa wichuraiana*, a Japanese prostrate rose which is very hardy, and the *Rosa multiflora* family, is a wilder species, usually more resistant to cold and more luxuriant. Its many branches spread from its trunk to form thick intertwining vegetation and under the right conditions it can grow very tall.

The flowers are not large and grow in clusters. They flower over a long period but only once a year, though often in great profusion. Given their great vitality, they should not be pruned. Beautiful and romantic, suitable for informal gardens, they are much loved in Great Britain.

Pruning

The new gardener is often confused about the pruning of roses. The most useful advice one can give regarding this operation, which has been learned through experience, is to use common sense. One rule is as good as another, except for a few simple basic principles.

Why prune?

a) To remove all the dead, diseased or dry wood; b) to replace branches that are too old with young, vigorous branches; c) to discourage excessive growth of branches and trunks so air can freely circulate; and d) for aesthetic reasons and questions of space.

When to prune

During periods of dormancy, before new growth begins; in colder climates, when there is no danger of frost.

Roses with a second flowering

(Hybrid Tea and Floribunda especially.) Newly established shrub roses should be heavily pruned the first year, but not climbers. For shrubs, cut the trunk back to only about 8 inches (20 centimetres) off the ground. Later pruning will be less drastic: cut back branches to about 10–12 inches (25–30 centimetres), possibly above a bud that you see on the base. It is important to be aware that hard pruning produces bigger flowers of better quality, while little pruning can mean a thicker shrub with smaller, less numerous flowers. Since the quality of flowers is less important in some rose bushes such as the Floribunda than it is in the Hybrid Tea and other Modern roses with large flowers, shrubs can be pruned to a height of 14 inches (35 centimetres).

Roses without a second flowering

Shorten the longer branches, trim the tangled lateral branches and dead wood; every 2–3 years remove the old branches to make way for healthy vigorous shoots. Species roses and their hybrids demand very little pruning; prune them to remove dead and diseased branches and to give them the shape you want according to how much space you have and the development of the plant.

Climbing roses

Before new growth starts, remove dead, twisted and undesirable branches; shorten the laterals but do not touch the main trunk. If the plant is too bare at the base, prune it low to encourage new shoots.

Ramblers

After flowering, prune back to the base almost all the branches that flowered, unless you are waiting for them to form rosehips. Remove dead and damaged wood when you can. For climbers and ramblers, it is important to remember that pruning can be divided into two categories: the first consists of rose bushes that produce flowers from new growth the same year, and the second is made up of those roses which produce flowers from the previous year's growth. Noisette roses, Hybrid Tea and Perpetual Hybrid roses all produce flowers from new growth on lateral branches that emanate from the main trunks. Thus their pruning should encourage the formation of these branches and also new main trunks that will eventually produce their own branches. In general, the rambler falls into the second category as do the hybrid roses like *wichuraiana*, *multiflora*, *sempervirens*, *arvensis* and also *banksiae*.

The Importance of Ash

Roses are not very difficult plants nor are they very demanding. They will grow in any type of soil, although they prefer it slightly acid, possibly of clay, with a pH between 6 and 6.5; however, they will also tolerate a slightly lime soil and will even grow in very poor sandy soil.

Plants of a temperate climate, with the exception of a few species and varieties, they tolerate both heat and cold fairly well as long as it is not excessive. They grow best in the sun but in hot climates also do well in partial shade. Different species and hybrid roses will even put up with full shade so long as it is not too dark, although their flowering will be less abundant.

As for feeding, to get good growth and luxuriant flowering it is necessary to enrich the soil with organic fertilizers once a year in the autumn and twice a year with chemical fertilizers based on potassium, phosphates and nitrogen. Nitrogen helps the development of the plants, phosphate favours the formation of roots and encourages flowering, and potassium increases their resistance to disease. Potassium is very important and can be given in the form of wood ash. Roses also need magnesium, as well as iron, which should be added to the soil at the first hint of chlorosis of the leaves.

Fertilizers should be given once after spring pruning and once more at the end of June. Do not overdo the amount of nitrogen given because it favours the development of foliage over flowers.

Diseases and Pests: their Prevention and Cure

The most common ailments affecting roses are mildew, rust and black spot.

Mildew is a mould resembling a light, ashy powder that covers the upper side of the leaf and can cause the plant to wither. It begins to develop in summer and some roses are more susceptible to it than others. It is not serious but should be kept under control so that it does not threaten the health of the plant. There are commercial fungicides available but they should be used with care because if they are sprayed at too close a distance, they can damage the foliage and branches.

Rust comes in the form of small orange-coloured patches rather similar to iron rust. Like mildew it establishes itself more easily when the climate is hot and very humid, but it is a more serious ailment. An attack of rust can eventually kill a plant. Upon maturation, the spores of this mould can dry out the leaves. Thus, at the first hint of infestation the infected leaves should be removed, carried away and burned, to insure that the spores do not remain inactive on other plants or on the ground and then reproduce the following year. Controlling them with fungicides is not very effective since rust strikes the underside of the leaf.

Black spot, which strikes Modern hybrids more than Old roses, is a fungus even more dangerous than rust. It shows up in the form of dark spots which indicate the death of the leaf tissue and it spreads rapidly until it withers all the foliage. Every leaf that falls contains hundreds and hundreds of spores ready to spread to other plants. To combat black spot, one proceeds in the same way as with rust, removing the diseased

[21]

leaves and burning them. Preventive measures include disinfecting the soil once a year with a preparation made for this purpose.

Among the insects that attack roses most frequently are aphids, small green or black parasites which completely cover the tender stems and buds. They are fairly innocuous but they give the plant an unattractive appearance and suck the sap. An excellent predator of aphids is the ladybird, which can be bought and spread in the garden to great advantage. Another ecological method is to remove the aphids manually the way it was done in the past, with a flat sponge or with little brushes sepcially for this purpose that look like a pair of sugar tongs.

Red spider mites tend to attack roses grown in greenhouses more than those grown in gardens. A serious infection of this

parasite is not common, but if your roses are infected, an old but efficient and non-toxic remedy is to sprinkle them with a solution of tar.

Caterpillars, the larval stage of various butterflies, live on roses before they metamorphose. In a few days they can get through a good deal of the foliage of a rose bush, leaving nothing but the skeleton.

Like the caterpillar, snails eat the foliage, leaving large round holes in the leaves.

It is never a good idea to rely only on chemical remedies. Spraying with a toxic substance always ends up damaging plants and poisoning the soil and the atmosphere, with the grave consequences we all know. Chemicals kill life indiscriminately, changing the ecological balance in nature.

For those who love roses and spend time caring for them every day or almost (and this is what one tends to do if one takes pleasure in growing roses), it is not difficult to pay attention and at the first hint of attack by pests, to combat them with methods which may not be very modern but are efficient. Caterpillars can be killed, if we can overcome our horror of them, by crushing them with a kitchen sponge, and snails can be eliminated with beer: just pour some beer into a tin and lean it against a log or a brick. The snails, lured by the smell, will crawl in and drown themselves.

OUT OF THE GARDEN: RECIPES

THE rose is not just a pretty flower. Earlier cultures appreciated the flowers and fruit for their medicinal value and extracted the precious oils from the petals. Folk medicine turned to the rose as a cure for many illnesses, especially those having to do with bodily fluids. It was also efficient in stopping bleeding and as a cure for diarrhoea, being astringent and anti-haemorrhagic because of its tannic acid content. Others used it to calm a cough, lower a fever, eliminate stones in the urine and cure rabies (something which in the past must have been of great concern since every herb was thought to have had such powers). The rose was also used in making cosmetics and in cookery.

If we begin with the Egyptians and follow the uses of roses until the end of the nineteenth century, there is a small legacy of recipes that tell how to make rose vinegars, oils, toilet waters, jellies, preserves, wines and syrups, infusions, sweets and pot-pourri. We owe two preparations to the Persians, who gave names that were destined to be used for a long time: '*julep*' for rosewater, and '*attar*' for rose perfume.

Searching in old herbalists' texts, in recipes or household accounts, we can make interesting discoveries. In England the following drink was quite popular under the Tudors and in the sixteenth century, when it was valued as a tonic and stimulant, excellent for both body and spirit: 'Prepare a brew with petals from the *eglanteria* rose, thyme, bayleaf and rosemary. For every 5 quarts [5.7 litres] of liquid, add 2 pounds [1kg] of honey. Leave it to steep for three days, pour it into a tub full of good beer and after another three days of rest, fill a keg. Wait for six months before drinking this miraculous potion.'

To be honest, a good part of these preparations, especially marmalades and preserves, do not manage to retain the unmistakable flavour of the rose: its perfume is often lost in the sugar. But a pot of jelly will preserve in its splendid ruby red colour the pleasant memory of a morning spent in the rose garden, filling a basket with sweetly scented petals.

The best roses to use for essential oils and in making cosmetics and food are the fragrant red ones, like the *gallica* and *damascena*, as well as some of the modern varieties, so long as they are very strongly scented. When using the hips, the best varieties are the *canina* and the *rugosa*.

The rose has been grown commercially since the eighteenth century for the extraction of its oils, in places like the Kazalink district of Bulgaria, in the south of France and near Paris, in England in Surrey and also in Turkey, Tunisia, Egypt and India. Today the use of the flowers by herbalists is rather limited. The most common commercial products today are rosewater, for use in cosmetics, as an astringent and as a tonic, and, in some countries, in confectionery, and rose oil. Rose essence is one of the oils used in many perfumes.

The fruit, in the form of rosehips, is an excellent source of vitamins, particularly vitamin C. For example, in 3½oz (100g) of orange pulp, there are 49mg of vitamin C, while in the same amount of rosehips there are between 230 and 700mg. One can make preserves, purées and broths with the hips, as well as a very good tea.

Rose Petal Jelly
apples – sugar – lemon – red rose petals

In a pot that can be tightly sealed, put red rose petals with the white part removed, until the pot is about one-third full. In a centrifuge or steamer, extract the juice of 7–9lb (3–4kg) apples, filter this and heat it with the juice of 1 or 2 lemons, and sugar in the proportion of 1½–1¾lb (750g) per quart (1.14 litres) of liquid. Remove the mixture from the heat as soon as it begins to boil and pour it into the pot. Seal it and keep it in a cool place.

Rosewater
11oz (300g) rose petals – water

Put the petals into a large pot, just cover them with water and boil for 3–4 minutes. This toilet water, which can be used as a refresher, a tonic and a mild astringent for the skin, will last for 3–4 days.

By adding them to the mixture before you boil it, you can also tint cotton, wool and lace a delicate antique rose colour.

Rose Oil
5 pints (3 litres) strongly scented rose petals – 1lb 2oz (500g) odourless vegetable oil

Put the petals into a stainless steel saucepan along with the oil and let the mixture steep for about an hour over a very low flame (or in the oven). Then let it cool and pour it into a glass container. Place it in the sun for four days, then filter it through fine cloth and bottle it. (The best containers would be small scent bottles.) Use a drop on the skin as a perfume or a tanning lotion. A few drops poured on to a piece of cottonwool can delicately perfume a cupboard. In some countries in the Middle East the oil is also used as a flavouring in fruit salads.

Rose Sugar
14oz (400g) rose petals – 2¼lb (1kg) granulated sugar

Put the petals and sugar in a bowl and mix them with your hands, breaking the petals into tiny pieces. Repeat this operation several times until the petals are completely crushed and almost transparent. Pour the mixture into a glass container and place it in the sun, tightly sealed, for about one month. Every so often, turn the container so it receives the sunlight evenly. Sift the sugar and put it into a clean container and seal it. This sugar can be used in confectionery, pastry making and to flavour fruit salads.

Crystallized Rose Petals
egg whites – rose petals – icing sugar

Mix a ½ teaspoon of cold water with each egg white used. Dip the petals into the egg white and then roll them in sugar. Arrange them on a sheet of greaseproof paper so they are not touching. Sprinkle them with a bit more sugar and then let them dry in the sun. After an hour, sprinkle them again and keep repeating this operation until they have hardened in the sun and the sugar has crystallized. Store them in a sealed container.

Rosehip Jelly
4 cups ripe rosehips – 2 small cups water – 2 cups sugar

Cut the fruit in half and take out the seeds with a spoon. Scrape away the fuzz. Boil the fruit in the water for half an hour. Then filter the liquid, add the sugar and bring it back to the boil until it reaches setting point.

Rosehip Tea
1 dozen rosehips – 1 pint (½ litre) water –
honey (optional)

Pour boiling water over the fruit, leave it for 8 minutes, then if required sweeten it with the honey; filter the liquid. Drink it hot before going to bed to fight colds and coughs or drink it cold as a thirst quencher.

Rosehip Purée

2¼lb (1kg) Rosa rugosa *rosehips – 4 cups water – juice from 1 lemon – sugar*

Remove the calyx and all the fuzz from the fruit. Cut them in half, and scrape out the seeds with a spoon. Boil the fruit in the water, stirring it until it is tender. Then force it through a food mill using the grid with the smallest holes. Add lemon juice and sugar to taste and serve it as a side dish to accompany a roast. It is also very good added to vegetable purées or to a soup.

Sir Hugh Platt's Pot-pourri

In his book *Delights for Ladies*, the sixteenth-century writer Sir Hugh Platt suggests the following method for making a rose pot-pourri, whose perfume should last 12 months. Fill an ovenproof pot with a layer of red rose petals 1¼in (3cm) thick. Put it in a warm oven for about an hour, stirring from time to time. Then leave it for another hour without stirring. When the petals are dry and still hot, put them in a terracotta pot, seal it with wax and hang it close to the fireplace. Open it when you want to release some of its scent into the room.

Rosewater for Sweets

Fill a tightly lidded pot with strong-scented rose petals, packing them in well. Add boiling water and let the mixture rest overnight, keeping the pot sealed. Filter the liquid and bottle it. Keep it cool and use it to flavour something sweet or to dress a fruit salad. It will keep for 2–3 weeks.

Rose-scented Honey

Follow the directions for Rosewater for Sweets. After filtering it, mix 1lb 2oz (500g) of the liquid with the same amount of honey. Let this rest for 2 weeks before using it.

ROSE BY ROSE:
A PERSONAL SELECTION

ALTHOUGH there are many roses about which I could write, I have chosen the ones that for different reasons I like best. Actually, there is one overriding reason: I find these particular roses beautiful, in fact, the most beautiful of all. I have painted them for the same reason and, for the same reason, the description that accompanies the pictures bears their name, even if, as you will see in reading this, they are part of groups with other examples which are also beautiful.

ROSA COMPLICATA

Of unknown origin, it is not, despite its name, a complicated flower at all. Experts maintain it is a hybrid between *Rosa gallica* and *Rosa canina*: a rose in any case not overly manipulated by humankind. It is a shrub but such a vigorous one that it can reach 8 feet (2½ metres) in height or width. It flowers profusely, once a year, with flowers of a moving beauty. They are large flowers, often reaching 4 to 5 inches (12 centimetres) in diameter, of a lively pink colour with white centres.

Because of its healthy, natural-looking appearance and its tolerance of shade, this rose grows very well in the most informal section of your garden, against a hedge that can gently support it, or at the edge of a wood or lawn. Under a tree, given enough space, it will reach up and embrace the trunk, putting out shoots and eventually forming a thick matting of green foliage that will burst into flower at the beginning of summer.

Like *Rosa gallica* in general, the old branches should be pruned every year so that vigorous new shoots develop. Shortening the shoots by a third is beneficial to the plant; it keeps the branches, when heavily burdened with flowers, from curving down to the ground. You can also thin the shrub if you like but it is not necessary. If the season has been very humid and oppressive, mildew can make a timid appearance, but it is probably best to ignore it. This is a robust rose that is not much affected by poor soil.

Rosa Complicata

CELSIANA

The group this rose belongs to was once called *damascena* because it was thought to come from the region of Damascus. Along with *centifolia* it was probably the only rose the ancients knew that had two flowering seasons. It merits attention not only for its beautiful blossoms but also for its intense scent, so intense in fact that it has gone down in history as the most fragrant rose.

For this reason it was widely cultivated by the Romans in the hinterlands of the gulf of Salerno for its essence. Though a bellicose and rough people they were nevertheless very sensitive to the charm of the rose, their favourite flower, which they always used to perfume their feasts and celebrations. One account tells how rose petals were used to make soft beds in the dining halls, and were dropped from the ceiling like rain. They were even known occasionally to smother a short senator. The Romans used rose oil as an oil with which to massage their bodies as part of their daily routine at the baths.

A variety of *damascena*, *damascena bifera* or autumn damask, boasts of one claim to fame: it was the only rose to bloom twice a year. Pliny tells of having seen it in flower in the autumn in the gardens of Paestum. When professional growers became aware of it at the beginning of the nineteenth century, they exploited this quality to create the first hybrids that bloomed more than once a year.

Besides its fragrance the *damascena* is beloved for its downy leaves, its blossoms, that seem to bend exhausted under the weight of their petals, and the free meandering growth of its branches (which makes it less suitable for the flowerbed but perfect when planted as a shrub among trees and meadow). Anyone who likes pink will love the many shades of this rose.

Which *damascena* should have the honour of being singled out first? Perhaps the **Celsiana**, a rose from the eighteenth century that is still found in gardens today. Its semi-double flowers with prominent gold stamens recommend it; its foliage is scented and of course the flowers themselves are very strongly perfumed; when the flowers open completely they can measure up to 4 inches (10 centimetres) in diameter, and they grow in clusters. Of an ethereal almost transparent pink, that fades into lighter tones streaked with silver, they are so delicate they seem made of crushed silk. They flower only once a year, abundantly, at the beginning of summer, and develop small slender fruit in the autumn that creates a very decorative effect.

A big shrub both in height and width, Celsiana can grow

Celsiana

up to 4 or 5 feet (1½ metres) in either direction. It is a genuinely charming shrub to add to a lawn, alone or mixed with other *damascena* or *Rosa gallica*.

With somewhat overblown double blossoms, **Ispahan** is another beautiful variety, first discovered in 1832. The shrub is more compact and contained than usual, with red flowers that are strongly scented.

Botzaris, developed in 1856, is considered somewhat difficult but of great quality and melting beauty, both for its flowers, which are not red this time but a pale cream dividing into quarters at maturity, and for its elegant light foliage.

Kazanlik takes its name from the region in Bulgaria where it is grown for its oils. This does not mean that it is not a superb garden rose as well. Its petals are a bit dishevelled looking when they open but this weakness does not detract from the plant at all. Because of their fragrance, they are the best roses for pot-pourris.

Mme Hardy for many years has been considered the most beautiful of the white roses. Its inner petals curve in towards a green centre that sits there like a precious stone lying on a bed of white cottonwool. The foliage is made up of cedar-coloured leaves, especially the newer ones.

St Nicholas is a late *damascena*, discovered by chance in 1950 in a garden in Richmond. It may be a spontaneous hybrid between a *damascena* and a *gallica* and its flowers take something from both. Semi-double, pink with golden stamens, it flowers only once a year, but it produces attractive fruit in the autumn and has blue-green foliage and thorny branches. Some books describe it as a strange rose but I do not know why. I find it beautiful.

CHAPEAU DE NAPOLEON

It is not easy to imagine a hairy, bearded rose and yet it exists. After all, there are bearded ladies, long-haired cattle and hairy cacti. In these roses, the part that is hairy is not the flower, but the buds, the sepals and the stems. And they really are hairy, covered with soft, downy, scented glands. Because the overall aspect of these glands looks like moss, these roses are referred to as moss roses. But they should not be confused with *Rosa moschata* which is a completely different rose, even if all of the very old roses are related.

The moss rose, and we must include one in our sampler, is a spontaneous mutation of *Rosa centifolia*, a rose that is not a species itself but a rather complicated hybrid which takes genes from many sources. Linnaeus baptized it *centifolia* but it would be more accurate to call it *centopetali*. Herodotus spoke of roses with sixty petals grown in King Midas's garden. According to historians and botanists over the centuries it was not common for roses to have sixty petals, so this rose as described by the ancients might have been *damascena*.

To enjoy real popularity, *Rosa centifolia* had to wait until the seventeenth century when the Dutch and also the French to some extent became aware of it and fell in love with it. They then produced one variety after another: between 1580 and 1700 they created more than 200. In turn, painters vied to immortalize it in voluptuous and languid-looking portraits; one of the most beautiful was painted by Fantin-Latour, the nineteenth-century French artist, and one of the most beautiful *centifolia* bears his name. In the nineteenth-century, it was the turn of *muscosa* to fill people with admiration, especially Victorian ladies and those who visited French gardens.

Zoe is a French rose from 1830 and it is very pink, with red, downy moss and narrow petals in the form of a flute, a lively addition to any garden. **Comtesse de Murinais**, dating back to 1843, is another French beauty, tall, with pale pink and cream flowers and green moss that has a rough texture and exudes an intense balsam-like fragrance. **Gloire des Mousseux** was born in 1852 with large pale flowers that curl in on themselves. The corolla is flat and divided into quarters, and the moss is a thick light green. Full of French charm and as sweet as its name is **Mousseline**, also called **Alfred de Dalmas**, a creamy, pink-coloured rose with delicate petals. It flowers first in June and then again later on, and its moss is a green laced with pink that eventually becomes rust coloured. Later in 1880, **Blanche Moreau**, arrived, heavily scented and still popular today. Although it is somewhat delicate and suffers from mildew, it is still loved for its pure white bloom and almost black moss. From Japan comes **Mousse du Japon** which has very hairy stems that look like the legs of a yak.

Chapeau de Napoleon, the oldest of them all is different. Discovered by chance in 1820 and then christened by Vibert in 1826, it is also called *Rosa cristata* because its moss is tufted. The buds are surrounded by full, fringed wings that grow from the calyx, so that they look rather like the three-cornered hat that Napoleon wore. The wings are so large that they seem to smother the bud inside them. Only about 4 feet tall (1½ metres maximum), this is not a very hardy rose and its slender branches seem hard pressed at times to support its flowers. It makes an attractive shrub to set in a mixed border among similar-sized plants. If it is an informal garden, the pale violet-pink colour of lavender and rosemary provides a good contrast; similarly the blue colouring of buddleia or ceanothus enhance this magnificent rose. It flowers in summer, first inspiring awe and enthusiasm with fantastic buds that adorn the bush like lace, then with intensely luminous, fragrant blossoms that start out round and then open flat and are divided into quarters.

Among the moss roses there is also a pillar rose which can reach 8 feet (2½ metres) in height. It has semi-double flowers of a light pink colour grouped in clusters. The foliage is dark and shiny and the moss a reddish brown. It is called **Jeanne de Montfort** and it flowers in summer.

Chapeau de Napoleon

ROSA CHINENSIS MUTABILIS AND ROSA X PAULII

As its name suggests, this is a Chinese rose, imported from an Asian garden, but its true origin is unknown. It is a sweetly extravagant rose that knows how to beguile: at times it is no more than a shrub 3 to 6 feet (1 to 2 metres) tall, at times it will spread along a protecting wall reaching a height of 20 feet (6 metres). But its fascination lies in the way it changes colour and in its flowers, which are smallish (only 2 inches/5 centimetres across) single flowers that blossom either singly or in small clusters. They start out as yellow or copper-coloured pointed buds, but when they open they can be a pale or an intense pink or orange or even streaked with colours. They can also turn crimson when they mature. The widely spaced petals give the corolla a light, fragile appearance. They are best in the morning when one can enjoy their freshness. In June the bush is covered with flowers, each with its own colour and in warm climates it continues to flower sometimes even until Christmas. The leaves are small, elegant and shiny with bronze-coloured shoots.

Not a bedding rose, it is most attractive at the edge of the garden where the formal flower garden gives way to a more untamed one.

Slow to start, lazy in its development, it might seem to be a weak plant. But give it time to settle in. It is very successful in temperate zones where its branches will eventually mature. In its first years, it should be pruned very little, and later, as space requires. It is a long-lived plant.

At the foot of *mutabilis* it is pleasing to let **Rosa x paulii** spread. The flowers of the two plants are similar, with petals that are not overly developed; they seem almost more like clematis than roses. The *Rosa x paulii* does not mind shade and it likes to trial along the ground. It is not a species but a hybrid, a cross between a *Rosa rugosa* and a *Rosa arvensis*. Its flowers are white, and pink in the lovely *rosea* variety, 3 inches (7½ centimetres) across, and lightly perfumed; it flowers in June. With its long, creeping shoots full of thorns, it can discourage the efforts of the gardener to remove it. But if you eliminate the branches that creep upwards you can create a very attractive contrast of heights with the two roses.

Rosa chinensis mutabilis

Rosa × paulii

MAIDEN'S BLUSH

It is hard for me to forgive a rose that is born pretty and tidy but ends its brief life tangled and not knowing where to put its petals. Unfortunately this happens to many roses and also somewhat to **Maiden's Blush**. But this particular rose never loses its charm or refinement; the fact that it does not have too many petals helps. If Maiden's Blush weakens with age, time does not destroy it and its youthful freshness lasts for all 'the space of its morning'. Its identity card says that it is a *Rosa alba*, a *Rosa alba incarnata* to be precise, and it has been around for several centuries. It is so strongly perfumed that when picked it can fill a room with its scent. Its semi-double flowers are lovely when they have just bloomed, and the still-curled petals hide an intense but tender pink. However the flowers are variable in colour and for this reason they have been called various suggestive names in the past, from 'virginal' to 'seductive', and even 'nymph's thigh' and 'emotional nymph's thigh'. Certainly it is one of the prettiest rose bushes that a garden can have today. The foliage is an elegant blue-green and the flowers, broad and abundant, are about 3 inches (7 centimetres) across. The bushes grow to a height of 5 feet (1½ metres) and flower once, in June and July.

In 1816 Maiden's Blush gave birth to a highly regarded offspring in the nursery of J Booth in England. In 1826 it was given the name **Königin von Dänemark**. A very densely petalled, carmine-coloured flower whose colour becomes softer when the buds open and divide into quarters, it is of medium size and sweetly scented. It blooms once in June and is a rose to be proud of.

Another *alba* is **Celeste**, a splendid rose with rounded blue-green foliage and large luminous pink blossoms that grow profusely in groups of two or three, with delicate, almost transparent, petals. It is called celestial I think because it must have belonged to the gods. A semi-double corolla, with small petals that curl up around the centre, first cuplike and then like a plate, it is definitely an old rose. After flowering, it is best to trim the branches that have flowered, and to prune it again when new spring growth begins to eliminate excess lateral branches.

Maiden's Blush

Rosa eglanteria, like *Rosa canina* and *arvensis* are roses we associate with childhood memories of joyful summer outings and first love. In dusty libraries of stately old homes, it is the eglantine that lies pressed between the pages of a novel, imprisoned there long ago.

Rosa eglanteria or *rubiginosa* has one outstanding characteristic: foliage that is small and graceful and gives off a strong odour of apples, especially after it rains. It has single, pink flowers that grow in clusters.

Commonly called the sweetbriar, Chaucer praised the gentle beauty of a hedge of these wild roses. Shakespeare, when he spoke of a rose, meant these. He advised among other things to grow them together with honeysuckle. By the end of the nineteenth century, *Rosa eglanteria* reached the peak of its fame when a certain Lord Penzance, a lawyer by profession, abandoned the law to devote himself body and soul to the eglantine, crossing and recrossing it with other roses popular at that time like the Hybrid Perpetual and the Bourbon rose, and throwing into the gene pool some genes from *Rosa foetida* or *Rosa harisonii* to stimulate its colour with their yellow flames. He thereby gave life to the rose known as Penzance Briar. Large shrubs up to 10 feet (2–3 metres) tall, and resistant to the cold, with many thorns, it is their fragrant leaves which give off the scent of apples.

They flower profusely but only in June, so it is necessary to enjoy their beauty quickly. Their very ephemeral quality though is part of what makes them beautiful. Thanks to these hybrids, *Rosa eglanteria* can enter our gardens in triumph and there are varieties for all tastes.

Lord Penzance has flowers in icecream colours, a single pink rose bathed in yellow, about 2 inches (5 centimetres) across, with lemon-yellow stamens. It is a less vigorous variety, usually not reaching more than 6 feet (1.8 metres) in height, thorny with very aromatic foliage.

Lady Penzance comes in the same shades but they are more decisive: the pink is stronger, tending towards salmon and copper. After flowering both husband and wife develop pretty round rosehips rich in vitamin C which beg to be made into infusions and jelly.

Amy Robsart bases its beauty on a rich pink blossom with a light-coloured centre. Its leaves are slightly less aromatic but when the shrub is in flower it is so fragrant it takes your breath away.

Even more intense are the shadings of the lovely and

Lord Penzance

cheerful **Meg Merrilees**, with scented, crimson, semi-double flowers. The foliage is also very fragrant, and the branches very thorny; the abundant rosehips turn a brilliant red.

If you want a delicate rose with dark veining, you might choose **Julia Mannering**. A rather vigorous shrub with semi-double large flowers, it would seem to deserve greater success. The same is true of **Green Mantle**, with its pinkish-red flowers, golden stamens and white centre.

The Penzance Briar, close as it is naturally and in appearance to species roses, should be planted in a less formal part of the garden and it should be planted alone. It works well in an informal garden, perhaps as a pretty hedge, mixed with honeysuckle as Shakespeare suggested, or as a big, green, flowery patch, or along a curving country path leading to a meadow or into a wood. This way, as you follow the path some spring morning after a rainfall, you can crush some of its aromatic leaves between your fingers while your eyes enjoy its flowers.

FRAU DAGMAR HASTRUP

Rosa rugosa, the group to which this hybrid belongs, comes from Japan, where it is called '*ramanas*', China and Korea. It is a plant which grows especially along the coasts, with large, strongly scented flowers that range from a lively pink to cherry red, foliage consisting of 5–9 small leaves that seem like coarse, wrinkled cloth and in the autumn with large, brightly coloured fruit. Knowing which is the true species is a problem because it is a rose of easy habits and it crosses with this one and that, producing lots of illegitimate offspring, some lighter and some darker. All, though, are thickly covered with thorns and a delightfully wrinkled foliage. The oldest of the hybrids recognized as legitimate and christened is **Blanc Double de Coubert** which reached Europe in 1892 with a corolla of immaculate whiteness and a very sweet scent. Its semi-double flowers blossom all summer. The shrub reaches a height of 6 feet (2 metres).

Another hybrid with pure white but single flowers is **Rosa rugosa alba,** one of the most beautiful of roses, with a fragrant flower about 4 inches (10 centimetres) across, very green foliage showing a defined veining, many grey-coloured shoots, and small grey thorns, thick as a forest. The hips are a shiny orange colour.

Queen of the group is **Frau Dagmar Hastrup (or Hartopp)**, a pale pink flower with streaks of silver and white; in the centre it has a tuft of cream-coloured stamens. It flowers from June onwards and bears apple-red, flask-shaped hips.

Scabrosa, discovered in England by Harkness in 1932 and registered in 1960, has enormous, cherry-red flowers with long stamens and hips that are so large they look like miniature apples. It is suitable for hedging.

Very special for the unusual shape of its flowers is the **Pink Grootendorst**, a *rugosa* that can hold centre stage all by itself. Although at first it may seem strange, you will come to love its small, double blossoms with fringed petals that resemble carnations, grouped in orderly clusters. It flowers often, and if the climate permits can be found blossoming as late as November. It also has a red version called **F J Grootendorst** and a white version, **White Grootendorst**. The first two are Dutch, the last was developed in the United States. But Pink Grootendorst is the sweetest of the three and offers the best of each of them, flowers that sometimes are pink, sometimes white and sometimes red.

Another variety that should not be forgotten is *Rosa x microrugosa*, a cross between a *rugosa* and a *Rosa roxburghii*.

It only blossoms once a year but we can forgive this because of its lovely flowers like crushed silk, of a transparent pink shading to lilac. It is the tallest of the group, growing up to 10 feet (3 metres) tall.

There are many good reasons to fall in love with these *rugosa*: for their abundant flowering, their healthiness and their robustness. They flower continuously, they have large, light blossoms nestled in deep, apple-green leaves, and they have a beautiful texture. They are resistant to everything: to frost and heat, to black spot, to mildew, to sheep who do not dare graze on their thorny branches, to blasts of wind, to shade.

The big rosehips that come in all shades of red, orange and crimson are formed quickly and can be found on the plant at the same time as the flowers, giving it a very decorative appearance.

It works well in a group; it will form long thick hedges which are almost impenetrable because of the intricate intertwining of branches and its many thorns. It can even tolerate being cut to the same level as boxwood – though they are not roses which require pruning, just an occasional clearing for those who want to prick themselves, and every two to three years a good pruning to remove dead wood and revitalize the plants.

In Norway almost every country house has a border of *rugosa*, of an enchanting green and clean lines. It even does well in the city, and in spite of pavements and cement it still manages to look beautiful.

Frau Dagmar Hastrup

TUSCANY SUPERB

Why is a rose called a rose if we always associate it with red? Maybe we like red roses because we associate them with love. But red, a suitable colour for silks and damasks, the colour of aristocratic thrones and theatre and train seats, seems somehow too heavy for a rose. Its fragile nature, which is the most basic quality of this flower, seems overcome by it.

And yet, how many garden arbours are cloaked in little vermilion-coloured roses and how many small gardens around offices and factories are adorned with triumphant red Comets, flame Big Bangs, red Pianetis, red Diavolos, scarlet Regines and Principesses and purple Cavalieris?

A cluster of little red roses, small and charming, can certainly bring a light hearted note to a sunny room. But one does not want to highlight the whimsy of the red rose by putting it triumphantly in the middle of the garden where it would be overbearing: instead one should put it somewhere more secret, next to a lush green that will calm the violence of its colour. For red roses should be velvety and satisfy dark and profound desires; they should have the dense thickness of blood, and guard an impenetrable mystery. There should be no yellow peeping out; all tones should be grave and nocturnal. You could choose the **Tuscany**, grown since medieval times, or the more recent variety **Tuscany Superb**, created in 1848 by William Paul with larger leaves and flowers and thicker petals. These are hybrids from *Rosa gallica*, to which we owe the most shining reds. Growing to a height of 5 feet (1½ metres) and good flowerers with open growth; the Tuscany Superb has large, fragrant, double and semi-double blossoms that come in a crimson that can look almost black in the creases, highlighted with touches of white towards the tuft of the stamens. Its scent is not the most intense but when it flowers in June it can seem almost excessive.

A very beautiful and intense red can also be found in the heavily perfumed **James Mason**, which has a long flowering period, and in **Sissinghurst Castle**, a brownish purple flower with a lighter underside and a rose which is especially pleasing to recall since it pays homage to the English writer-gardener Vita Sackville-West, who grew it in her splendid garden at Sissinghurst in Kent. Another *gallica* purple, this time with undertones of violet, is **La Belle Sultane**.

Tuscany superb

CORNELIA

Between 1925 and 1930, after years of intensive work, a group of splendid roses was born in the nursery of an English minister, Joseph Pemberton. All the roses were descendants of a species of *Rosa moschata*, and all were destined for lasting success. Most of them bear the names of women: Cornelia, Penelope, Francesca and Felicia, as well as Vanity and Moonlight. They are shrub roses with smallish flowers clustered in dense masses at the end of long downward-curving branches. They have all the ingredients for success: they are graceful, and flower perpetually in a range of pastel colours, and have a light, musk-scented perfume. They belong in a meadow or near a lawn where they do well in small intertwining groups; this plays up the individual qualities of each in harmonious interplay. They also make attractive small hedges.

Cornelia is a shrub that can grow up to 6 feet (2 metres), with foliage that turns bronze in the autumn. The first flowers arrive in June and July, though in warm climates they may come out in May. It flowers again in the autumn, this time with larger and more intensely coloured flowers. The flowers are semi-double and double, in a delightful colour defined as pale coral or copper-pink with yellow undertones; they start out an apricot colour that gradually becomes pinker. The plant later develops a good number of small red fruit.

Felicia resembles Cornelia. It has strongly scented double flowers, that are larger, and in a cooler pink that is almost silvery. The shrub is more compact and leafy and blooms continuously.

Penelope is the most popular, with even larger flowers (though there are always many smaller ones as well). It is intensely perfumed with semi-double flowers that fade from pink to cream and are flat when open. Penelope blossoms most heavily in June and July and if the dead flowers are removed, will continue to blossom abundantly. In the autumn, a single cluster might consist of a hundred flowers. These are followed by small red fruit.

Vanity has almost single, deep pink flowers that smell like sweet peas. They are more lax in their growth and have a fine autumn flowering.

Moonlight has cream-coloured semi-double flowers with golden stamens and a very pleasant, musk-scented perfume.

Francesca is yellow, but it is a strong apricot-yellow. It has robust rigid branches and rather large semi-double flowers with shiny, dark green foliage.

Eva is not a Pemberton rose, but it is still a *moschata* hybrid.

Cornelia

Developed by Kordes in 1938, it brings to the group a carmine-red note which is paler towards the centre and turns white just before reaching the yellow stamens. The single, beautifully shaped flowers are a bit larger than normal and have a sweet scent.

One last red is the **Sadler's Wells**, which comes from Penelope and is a very recent and interesting creation of Peter Beales, an English rose-grower. A perpetually flowering shrub that reaches a height of 4 feet (1.2 metres), it is a very tidy plant with lightly scented, semi-double flowers that bloom in clusters, yet remain separate. They have an unusual colour: the petals start out a silvery pink and end up cherry-red at the tips. An excellent autumn-flowering rose, it can withstand all kinds of weather. These make attractive cut flowers.

The hybrids of *Rosa moschata*, if left unpruned except in spring, become quite thick, with arching branches. A system used in England to control the powerful lateral shoots is to stake them to the ground. Removing some of the faded flowers reduces the number of rosehips but it favours the development of new shoots that will produce other flowers later. Watch out for an attack of mildew in the autumn and treat it promptly.

FRÜHLINGSMORGEN AND FRÜHLINGSGOLD

The *Rosa pimpinellifolia* which up until a few years ago was called *spinosissima* has a right to both names: certainly it is very spiny. Bristling with all kinds of thorns and prickles, there does not seem to be a spot on its branches that is deprived. However *pimpinellifolia* is another name for the aromatic herb *Sanguisorba* or burnet and *spinosissima* is also called by this name because it is thought that there is a resemblance between the lovely, small, delicate foliage of the two plants. The flowers of *spinosissima* are white or pale pink and the fruit changes from red to a deep brown to black, with surprising effect.

It is found throughout a vast region, from southern Europe to Iceland, and from Russia to China. Since it is found along the coastal regions of Scotland, in England it is sometimes called the Scottish rose.

In fact, the Scots have created and registered almost 300 varieties, with single and double blossoms in magnificent colours. But although such hybrids have remained mostly confined to British gardens, other Modern roses, created by Kordes in Germany and derived from the same rose, have become very popular everywhere. All have remained faithful to the name they were given – 'Frühling' (spring).

Frühlingsgold was the first, born in 1937. A large, healthy bush, it needs plenty of space for its long branches; along them blossom its famous 'spring gold' flowers. Semi-double, golden corollas up to 5 inches (12 centimetres) across, they announce their presence from a long way off by their intense perfume that fills the air. Their visit is brief, however, for they only flower during the month of May. Occasionally, however, Frühlingsgold is kind enough to return with a late second flowering.

Frühlingsmorgen (spring morning), born in 1942, offers a little more. It has compact foliage, large single blossoms that are cherry-pink on the outer edges and change to yellow near the stamens – which open like a golden yellow halo. They are deeply fragrant and have a second flowering. In the autumn they produce dark purple fruit.

The same year, 1942, **Frühlingszauber** (spring enchantment), arrived. A charming crimson fading to a silvery pink, it is fragrant and produces fruit. **Frühlingsduft** (spring perfume) was developed in 1949 and has lemon-yellow and apricot, double flowers. One last rose, the **Frühlingsanfang**, is truly a lovely 'beginning of spring', and it also makes a lovely autumn plant with bronze and copper leaves and brown fruit. The flowers are a strongly scented ivory, about 3 inches (7 centimetres) across.

Among the Frühling group it is hard to know which to choose, but one should certainly choose at least one. Better still, take one of each and give them free rein. They grow well anywhere, even in sandy soils, and they will tolerate partial shade. Gertrude Jekyll, who was very instructive about where to plant roses, advises planting these roses next to a stairway and letting them follow the line of the banisters up the stairs, or at the top of a grassy slope so that they grow down it and cover it – she considered such grassy slopes ugly. The roses, she wrote, 'throw themselves down headlong showing themselves capable of grace and elegance'.

Frühlingsmorgen

Frühlingsgold

GOLDEN WINGS

Among the hybrids of *spinosissima* two roses deserve a place in the garden: you will not regret planting them. One is **Stanwell Perpetual** which came from the nursery run by Mr Lee in Stanwell, Middlesex. It is a shrub with long, thorny, meandering branches, suitable for training around a tree. It has two characteristics that some consider defects, but others consider signs of elegance: one is that it has rather slender branches and the other is that its foliage has a tendency to develop purple spots. A favourite of Miss Jekyll's, she advises planting three of them 1 foot (30 centimetres) apart so that their twisting branches can support each other. As for the purple spots, I think they are charming. It is a rose that is beautiful in every way, with blood-red thorns, light grey-green foliage made up of nine elements, an excellent fragrance, and small clusters of shell-pink, semi-double, slightly ruffled flowers with a pretty centre, that are about 3 inches (7.5 centimetres) across. Later these turn a paler shade. The plants flower at the beginning of June and then because they are descendants of the autumn-flowering *Rosa damascena*, they flower again in November. Stanwell Perpetual should be pruned after it first blossoms and then again at the end of winter.

The other hybrid that deserves special attention is **Golden Wings**. It is a rose which keeps the promise of its name: its curling petals seem like unfurled wings, though they are not actually golden, but a more transparent pale yellow. A shrub that can reach a height of 6 feet (2 metres), it can also be grown as a pillar rose, by winding it around a column. Created in America in the 1950s, it does not stop flowering from May to October, producing light yellow flowers that are darker towards the centre where a tuft of red filaments and copper-coloured anthers burn. The scented corollas are single with a few extra petals; almost 5 inches (12 centimetres) across, they seem very large when open, although they tend to close in the evening. Golden Wings also likes to wander and it can be tiresome trying to keep it tidy. Prune it back by about one-third.

Golden Wings

GEORGE VIBERT

Roses and other flowers with variegated, striped or spotted petals may seem like freaks of nature. Perhaps they are and there are many who do not like them. But **George Vibert** (Robert, 1853) – an old *Rosa gallica*, if not the oldest variegated rose (that is *Rosa gallica versicolor*, very famous in the ancient world and in the Middle Ages) – wins our sympathy because it has a graceful and refined whimsy. It has tender pink, light red, white or timid cherry stripes that lie side by side or cross quietly, producing no violent contrasts. Its many petals open in a somewhat disorderly manner but they never go too far. It forms an erect, compact bush with an attractive shape, reaching a height of 3 feet (1 metre). The smallish flowers blossom in the summer with varying colours, depending on climate (something that is true in general of variegated roses). Given their modest size, they can also be grown in pots or they can form small hedges or work as part of a group. They also do well in rock gardens and are easily grown even in poor soil.

For those who delight in this capricious group, I will mention some of the more extravagantly coloured roses. **York and Lancaster** or *Rosa damascena versicolor* is of unknown origin but was certainly seen in gardens long before the sixteenth century. Semi-double and fragrant, it can have white petals, pink petals and striped petals with an all-pink or all-white corolla. An attention getter, it is a tall shrub which flowers in the summer.

Among the *Rosa muscosa* there are also some variegated species, namely the **Oeillet Panachée**. Among the Modern roses, **Picasso**, developed by McGredy of New Zealand, stands out as a Floribunda with abundant flowers: its nickname, 'Hand-painted rose', suits it. Its corollas are cherry-red with white smudges in the centre and a few white spots; on the reverse side it has cherry and white stripes.

George Vibert

BALLERINA

Ballerina was born in England but it is not known exactly from which rose. It is possibly a hybrid of *Rosa moschata* but it might also belong to the Floribunda group. However, it does not much matter. A rose of delicate beauty, it is mistakenly used by gardeners as a bedding rose when instead it deserves a special spot so that its gentle grace is not lost. A rose that can be kept confined to a pot, it has small, almost tiny, pink flowers that change to magenta and have a white centre; as they mature their colour fades till they are white. On a pretty bush with light green leaves, they do not even look like roses; they look more like small groups of butterflies. Ballerina blossoms all summer and continues on until autumn when it develops small orange fruit.

One way to appreciate it is to grow it close to another Modern rose, **Erfurt**, possibly even more showy. Created by Kordes in Germany in 1929, it is about the same height, 3 feet (1 metre) tall, with curved shoots that are red when young. It flowers at the same time, from the middle of June onward, with more fragrant, larger flowers that are very light semi-doubles with the same shading of colours, pink-magenta that whitens over time. In the white centre there is a tuft of mustard-yellow stamens.

Ballerina and Erfurt are resistant to the cold but also can be grown successfully in hot climates where they like partial shade. Follow the rules for the Frühling roses when pruning.

Ballerina

NEVADA AND MARGUERITE HILLING

Nevada is an excellent specimen of a Modern shrub. Though it is a Modern, born in 1927, its appearance is delightfully old fashioned. Developed in Spain by Pedro Dot, its origin is not entirely clear although we know from its creator that it is a cross between *Rosa moyesii* and a Hybrid Tea rose. Its long flexible branches that grow up to almost 6 feet (2 metres), are literally weighed down with gorgeous creamy white flowers in June. The single flowers are up to 5 inches (12 centimetres) across, with one or two petals curling in towards the stamens; in colder climates they are flushed with pink. They bloom intermittently throughout the summer, though not as abundantly as the first blossoming. Nevada's only drawback is that it has no scent.

Marguerite Hilling is a spontaneous mutation from Nevada and they are attractive grown together. It was discovered in the 1950s contemporaneously in three different nurseries in England and New Zealand. Marguerite Hilling has slightly smaller but abundant flowers which, like Nevada, do not blossom quite as profusely after the first time. A pink that gets darker towards its centre, the colour looks as if it has been daubed on with a paintbrush.

Feed these two roses regularly so that they can flower as profusely as nature will allow them. In some regions they are susceptible to black spot. To help Nevada and Marguerite Hilling maintain their beauty and their bountiful flowers over a span of years, it is necessary to be ruthless and every two to three years rigorously eliminate all the old wood.

Marguerite Hilling

Nevada

WARWICK CASTLE

If we read the catalogue of David Austin, one of the best rose-growers in England, we may feel our rose garden is lacking a very important group of roses, one we really must not do without. David Austin calls these roses 'English roses'; I do not know why, but they do seem truly English. Their excellence consists in their having inherited the best qualities of their parents, an Old rose crossed with a Modern, a Hybrid Tea or Floribunda. From the first parent, we get delicacy and grace, fragrance, shape and old-fashioned style; from the second, infinite shadings and the ability to continue blooming. The group is large – generally small-sized shrubs – and I frankly do not know which one to choose. I would like to be queen and own them all.

Warwick Castle is one example of the English rose. It has an intensely pink, almost transparent, corolla, lit up as if by a small flame, with a rich scent, and petals arranged like a geometric rosette on gently curving branches. Like many roses in this group, it is less than 3 feet (80 centimetres) tall, and thus well suited for small gardens.

Wife of Bath, created in 1969, has flowers like Sèvres porcelain cups, in pink fading to white, and perfumed like myrrh. It is a leafy bush with many twisting branches and is quite hardy despite its very refined appearance.

The thick petals of **Claire Rose** are always pink at the centre and white at the edges. Arranged elegantly in quarters, the corollas look like they have been cut from fine vellum.

Never without a flower, the petals of **Mary Rose** are pinker and less carefully arranged than the others and have a lovely *Rosa damascena* fragrance.

Walter Raleigh, a hot pink, bears its name proudly: its unique, peony-like flowers are curly and fringed, with a tuft of golden stamens at the centre.

There is also an apricot-painted yellow variety, **Perdita**, with its petals divided into quarters and a heavenly fragrance that deserves a medal.

These roses have no special growing needs but, being abundantly flowering species, they should be kept well fed. Pruning is the same as for other reflowering species.

Warwick Castle

RED BLANKET

There are not many gardens where you find roses covering the ground like a carpet. In fact, it is quite unusual to find a naturally prostrate rose. But there are some. These grow in spurts, a little taller here, a little shorter there, and they begin to stretch and creep over everything they come across – sprawling along the ground here, crossing over walls and rocks there. Some cover only a few feet (a metre or so) of ground, others advance over several.

This rose is the flower equivalent of the basset-hound. It is truly a low-growing rose. Roses like the *moschata* hybrids or the Frühling roses like to hurl themselves gracefully down a cliff or over a slope with their flexible branches. But a real prostrate rose like the **Max Graf** actually spreads over the ground if it finds the right place. Vertically, it grows no higher than 1½ feet (50 centimetres) but horizontally it can cover a radius of 8 feet (2½ metres) with thick, bright green foliage smelling of apples. It blossoms in early spring and has beautiful, single flowers that are a deep pink with a light centre; only rarely does it produce fruit. It is a hybrid from a *Rosa rugosa* and a *Rosa wichuraiana*, and of American origin.

Nozomi on the other hand was created in Japan and it is such a low-growing plant that there is no way to make it taller unless you train it up a form and then let it cascade down in a fall of bright green leaves. Everything about Nozomi is delightful and tiny: small green leaves which sometimes turn a bit bronze, tiny flowers like little strings of pink pears, and tiny orange fruit. It flowers abundantly but only once, in early spring.

Red Blanket is not so low: it can grow 2–3 feet (60–80 centimetres) tall and create a thick bush that will spread over a large area, forming a big, beautiful cushion of rather large, deep pink, almost red, single flowers. It has two important qualities: year-round foliage and repeated flowering. If you prefer a different-colour cushion, with smaller but still abundant flowers, try **Rosy Cushion.**

Very popular among the prostrate roses is **Snow Carpet**, created by McGredy in New Zealand. It is not a true creeper but a miniature that amasses small branches with little leaves on which rest a snowfall of tiny flowers in the summer. They are very double and very white. The plant grows to a height of 1½–3 feet (45–90 centimetres). The **Swany** is also a white double. An excellent rose, with bronze-coloured foliage, it reaches a height of 3 feet (90 centimetres).

Of the other species, *Rosa x paulii* is also prostrate, growing

Red Blanket

to about 3 feet (80 centimetres) tall, as is *Rosa wichuraiana* which produces vigorous shoots up to 10 feet long (3 metres), *Rosa richardii* and *bracteata*.

These roses have no special requirements, except for enough space to allow them to show off their beauty: a rock garden is good, as well as at the base of other bushes; at the edge of a lawn; to fill in a space between some other rose bushes; to cover a slope; or to follow the steps of a rustic footpath. They can also cascade from a pot.

Generally they do not require pruning except when necessary to keep the bush clean and tidy.

ANNA PAVLOVA

No rose is more unnatural than a Hybrid Tea, yet many people consider it the rose *par excellence*. Many do not even realize that there are any other kinds. The Hybrid Teas receive the most attention in catalogues, and nurseries give them all the publicity they can muster. They are large with long straight stems perfect for cutting, and majestic heads in dazzling indelible colours with infinite shadings: magenta with a reverse side of yellow, yellow with a reverse side of crimson, cream suffused with magenta, silver edged in carmine, a red so deep it is almost blue-black. They are flowers which from a commercial standpoint are perfect. They are so perfect in fact that they are only really grown for their flowers. The flowers are indeed impressive and they do bloom constantly. But, on the other hand, perhaps the reason that people grow them so often and love them so much is because they are the best known and they are the best known because they are showy, they are constantly in flower and they are easy to get started.

However, I do not want to condemn the whole lot. Among the Hybrid Tea roses created in the first thirty years of this century, there are some that still recall their noble antecedents. Both mutations of the celebrated **Ophelia, Mme Butterfly**, in many shades of pink with a lemon-yellow centre, is always splendid, as is **Lady Sylvia** with beautifully shaped buds, an exquisite fragrance and a flesh-pink blossom. Two more worthies are **Lady Waterlow**, a hardy French climber with a semi-double, pink blossom, and **Shot Silk**, an old favourite of Nordic gardens, in a shade between pink and yellow found nowhere else.

The most recent Hybrid Teas – and new ones are served up every year, pushing earlier ones into the background – have rather complicated genealogies and the genes from *Rosa thea*, between one cross and another, have been lost. Their name in fact has more correctly become 'Modern rose', and they are listed as 'Shrub roses with recurrent large flowers'. In the last fifty years, there have been some colossal successes among these flowers: **Peace**, certainly the biggest success, has become famous all over the world. Many bear the names of VIPs – princesses, singers, screen stars, presidents, even stars in the sky. There is **Charles de Gaulle**, **Princesse de Monaco**, **Cathérine Deneuve** and **Orion**, as well as more anonymous names like **Dorabella**, **Mirella** and **Colombina**. Each one has its own colour, a beautifully shaped bud or corolla, and long, sturdy stems.

If I had to choose one among these roses, I would choose

Anna Pavlova, created in England in 1981 by Peter Beales who has lost the flower's genealogy. So it is an orphan, but an undisputable beauty. The flowers are of a very pale, rather cool, pink colour, almost ash-coloured in fact, like old silk, with darker shading where the petals overlap, and gently undulating edges. The corollas stand erect on their stems and are intensely perfumed. Peter Beales advises against pruning the plants (even though shrub roses usually need drastic pruning), leaving them to develop a large thick bush with abundant green foliage.

There are other Hybrid Tea roses that are particularly beautiful which do not resemble the classic example at all: they have large but single corollas, with shell-pink scalloped edges like the charming **Dainty Bess**, or of golden yellow and orange like **Mrs Oakley Fisher** or pure white with crimson anthers as in **White Wings**, a fragrant rose with long, elegant, pink buds.

Anna Pavlova

LILAC CHARM

Created by LeGrice in England in 1961, this belongs to the Floribunda group. Commonly known as bouquet roses, these are the Modern shrub roses that are grown triumphantly in small public and private gardens, and in orderly city flower-beds. They are the roses planted *en masse* to create special colour effects with their constant even overwelming flowering. I personally prefer not to be hit over the head by an avalanche of red or yellow or pink, but would rather be forced to wait for a flower to open, so that one morning there among the green appears a single precious blossom whose fresh beauty gives us brief but intense pleasure. **Lilac Charm** falls into this category, a flower of quality, enchantment and even a light scent. Its prettily shaped almost single flowers are an unexpected and delicate lilac-mauve, warmed by red filaments in the stamens and by amber-coloured anthers. It is a low compact shrub, about 2 feet (60 centimetres) tall, with dark green, opaque foliage. The blossoms, if cut when they are still buds and placed in a glass vase with water, will open very gracefully.

When pruning, follow the guidelines for continuously flowering roses. Cut them low when they start to grow again in the spring but not as much as for roses with large flowers.

Of the Floribundas I can recommend **Escapade**, with semi-double, musk-scented, magenta-pink flowers with pale centres. It is constantly in flower, blossoming on and on until the end of the autumn, as does **Iceberg** or **Schneewitchen** – from Kordes. Highly prized, Schneewitchen is an excellent bedding rose for those who love a rose that is as white as the snow. It has a lovely sweet scent, glossy, light foliage, and a semi-double, medium-sized blossom that opens flat when fully mature. Iceberg can be mixed successfully with Escapade or Lilac Charm and it also makes an attractive low hedge in a green meadow. There is a climbing form too, but if it does not come from a good cutting it will not produce many flowers.

Sarabande has received five prizes, confirming its success. Another Floribunda, a French one this time from Meilland, it has bright orange, semi-double flowers. It has little scent but is very effective when you want to add a splash of colour.

Lilac Charm

ROSA BRACTEATA

In 1793 Lord Macartney left for China on a diplomatic mission. What he did in China does not matter much. What does matter is that he returned home with a fine gift for Europe, the *Rosa bracteata*, also known as the Macartney rose. It does need a temperate climate, but will grow in England in sheltered areas.

It is a magnificent plant. Its buds are surrounded by full green bracts, its large silk-like corollas are perfectly shaped, its long stamens flutter in the breeze like yellow flames. It has a fruity scent, with year-round, small, emerald-green leaves that form a beautiful thick mantle. It sends out vigorous shoots that crawl up a wall or along the ground, reaching lengths of 12–15 feet (4–5 metres).

It is a very useful rose when you have bare ground that needs covering or a desolate part of the garden that needs filling in, either horizontally or vertically. The sight of a single flower, which continue to appear from July to November, can make your heart beat with pleasure. It is not the right plant for the gardener looking for the grand effect, but for someone who wants a healthy, natural beauty, it is a joy.

Rosa bracteata has only produced one hybrid so far, **Mermaid**, but it is a charmer and could be called a climbing version of Golden Wings. Its very large, scented, single flowers, that grow individually and up to 6 inches (15 centimetres) across. These open up like plates, and are a light yellow, somewhere between cream, sulphur and lemon, with a warm pompon of amber-coloured stamens that decorate the plant even after the petals have dropped. In a sheltered position, the plant is evergreen; if next to a northern wall, it will lose its foliage but will still grow to heights of more than 25 feet (8 metres). It flowers late in the summer but will continue to flower in the autumn, later producing clusters of flowers as well.

Mermaid does not like frost nor does it like transplants. Once it has been planted it is necessary to give it time to settle in; it may be a year before it starts to grow. It is a good idea to stake the shoots when it is young. If you have room, do not prune it except to remove dead or damaged branches. Mermaid is sterile and rather difficult to reproduce.

Rosa bracteata

ROSA X ANEMONOIDES AND
ROSA X DUPONTII

Rosa x anemonoides only blooms once, between May and June, but it is enough. As its name suggests, its large flowers resemble anemones. Flat, with overlapping petals, they are shell-pink veined with a darker pink. When they open, each petal is like a heart. It is an enchantingly shaped flower. The foliage is somewhat sparse and the branches, which can reach 13 feet (4 metres), are rather bare. It is a hybrid of German origin, developed in 1895 from a *Rosa laevigata*, probably crossed with a *Rosa thea*; but of the tea scent only a hint has remained. What is stunning about this plant is the fragile trembling beauty of its flowers, a beauty that more showy roses must certainly envy.

Rosa x dupontii, if asked, would surely say that it would be happy growing at the feet of *Rosa x anemonoides*, to cover the bare ground beneath it with its green foliage and keep the pink flowers of *anemonoides* company with its own white ones. It is another rose with a short genealogy, rather similar to a species. It comes from a cross between *Rosa moschata* and perhaps *Rosa damascena*: Mr Dupont, who in 1817 made history by giving it his name, was a lucky man. It was grown at Malmaison and Rédouté honoured it by painting its portrait (giving it the name *Rosa damascena subalba*), but it was certainly grown before that. It flowers a little later than *anemonoides*, between June and July, and though it does not actually reflower, it sometimes puts out a few more blossoms. The luminous single corollas with sometimes six sometimes eight overlapping petals, measure 3–4 inches (7–9 centimetres) across and are elegantly drawn; the branches, with few thorns, reach 6½ feet (2 metres) and carry soft pink buds. After it finishes flowering, a subtle coral-coloured fruit sometimes appears.

To complete this idyll, try letting a clematis grow amongst the other two, a Perle d'Azure for example, that would add its cool blue to the pink and white of the others.

Rosa × *anemonoides*

Rosa × *dupontii*

MEG

Meg is a name that is too familiar for a rose with such distinction and presence. Its very regular, slightly semi-double flowers are shaped like a Tea rose, large, flat and gently curving. It is a genuine climber, capable of growing up to 13 feet (4 metres). I can easily imagine its elegant, scented flowers and dark, shiny green foliage adding softness to an old wall, creeping along faded, yellowing plaster. It is a salmon-apricot colour that fades to apple pink with streaks of a rosy peach. In its centre its reddish-orange stamens look like glowing embers. After a first flowering in the middle of June, it has a second though less abundant one later. Its branches should be staked securely to whatever framework it is to be grown upon, be it an arch or a pergola, as they are rather fragile; care should be taken that they do not break.

If the walls of your house are of white plaster, a more delicate effect can be achieved with another climber similar to Meg but with larger flowers and a unique shape, having semi-double petals that are wavy and fold back. This is **Cupid** with sweeter, cooler shades of flesh-pink suffused with apricot. Fragrant and vigorous, it grows to over 13 feet (4 metres). It flowers only in June but later it puts out large orange-coloured fruit in clumps that stay on the plant all winter.

For those who like white and the effects of white on white, there is **Silver Moon**, created in America from a cross between two species, a *Rosa wichuraiana* and a *Rosa laevigata*. Luxuriant and exuberant like both its parents, it grows to over 19 feet (6 metres); from *laevigata* it gets pretty, shiny, delicate, green foliage. It flowers from the middle of June, producing cream-coloured buds and white, single or semi-double flowers as airy and fleeting as moonbeams. Their uniquely shaped petals, enclosing golden stamens, lie on silvery grey branches and give off a scent that reminds one of apples.

Meg

COCKTAIL

If you have a garden with a small, rustic wall that needs some colour, try growing a climber either up it or, even better, cascading down from above. **Cocktail** is a good variety to turn to. Created in France in 1959 by Meilland, the famous hybridist who has given us many varieties including Peace, Cocktail, which can grow up to 5 feet (1.5 metres) in height or width, is well suited to the part of the small climber, crawling up or trailing down a wall. But it also does well, when left free, in a lawn, where it will grow in all directions. It flowers and reflowers abundantly, in clusters or singly, with dazzling single flowers 2–3 inches (5–7 centimetres) in diameter in a lively scarlet that grows darker as the flowers mature. The heart-shaped petals open flat revealing a centre that can be white or yellow. Although it has a light scent, that is not what makes it endearing. It is instead its cheerful, sprightly appearance, pleasantly unrefined and countrified, that makes one fall in love with it.

In regions that are hit by frost, Cocktail has a tendency to die back to the base and then put out new shoots at the beginning of spring. Strong wind can also damage it as its wood is somewhat fragile.

If you are the sort of person who thinks that the only colour for a rose is pink, and that red is too strong a colour for such a plant, do not worry. You can cover your wall with another rose from Meilland that has most of the same characteristics as Cocktail with the exception of its colour and it even grows a little taller: 10 feet (3 metres). This is **Clair Matin**, an appropriate name for a flower that is as fleeting as a crystal clear morning. Its colour seems to be stolen from the dawn: a tender pink, at times it is warmer and orangier in tone and at times it is a cool, pearly pink. This plant can truly lighten up a morning. It flowers continuously until autumn, with medium-sized, single flowers, and with the most important quality in a pink rose, a delicate, flowing grace. The branches are chocolate coloured and the leaves when young tend towards bronze.

Clair Matin should be kept pruned, and dead flowers and twisted branches removed; prune it by shortening the lateral shoots and the main branches, where necessary, at the beginning of spring.

Cocktail

ROSA BANKSIAE

There is a huge choice of roses to train around an arch or a doorway or to grow over a pergola or cover the walls of a house. But no other kind can do it better than the ramblers. The rambler, thanks to the tangled blossoming of its vegetation, the soft, fluid growth of its branches, and its thick, flowing mantle of flowers, gives the pergola and gazebo a gentle, natural appearance, masking their hard, angular edges. In nineteenth-century gardens there was always a pergola with *Rosa banksiae* growing over it and this is why we think of these roses with such nostalgia, as if they could take us back to the romantic past.

Originally from China, the true species was from the mountains, with single, cream-coloured, strongly scented flowers but no one knew or grew it. The first variety to arrive in England from Canton was *Rosa banksiae banksiae* or *banksiae alba plena*, a giant able to reach a height of 50 feet (15 metres), with very white, double flowers with fat, violet-scented tassles. The two yellow varieties are more popular. Of the two *banksiae lutea* is grown more often and has more abundant flowers with a ruffly, butter-yellow rosette; although it is more abundant, it has less of a scent. The other, *banksiae lutescens* has very pretty, single, pale flowers that have a delightful scent. They all flower in May and June and afterwards can be enjoyed for their dense foliage and their smooth, spineless branches. The old wood turns a golden brown and is covered with a subtle, transparent film.

Even though they grow at an altitude of 50,000 feet (1,500 metres) in the wild, they do not much like cold, though they do well in most parts of England. Their favourite spot is against a wall that gets the midday sun. They do not like to be moved; to make them more malleable some growers graft them on to other trunks. Be careful with pruning: they flower from old branches, not from new shoots. Thus, you should remove the dry wood but never trim the main branches while the plant is young. Some can be removed once the plant is 4–5 years old to make way for new growth.

Rosa banksiae banksiae

Rosa banksiae lutescens

ROSA FILIPES KIFTSGATE

Rosa filipes Kiftsgate behaves much like *Rosa banksiae*, and is another Chinese climbing rose that came to Europe at the beginning of this century. It grows triumphantly, spreading its shoots over everything it comes across. This variety owes its names to the area in the Cotswolds where perhaps the largest specimen in the world exists. In July when it is at its peak, this reaches a height of 59 feet (18 metres) and a width of 46 feet (14 metres), releasing a bursting cascade of cream-coloured buds and lighter, single, not very large flowers (only 1½ inches or 4 centimetres across). But what does it matter how small the flowers are, when in a single cluster, its owner has counted 428 blossoms?

Its perfume bursts from the styles of the pistils fused together to form columns. Flowering in the early summer and then not again until the following year, it has grey-green foliage made up of 5–7 small leaves that turn golden in the autumn. It also produces an orange fruit.

If you have a large, bare tree, wooden hut or old wall to cover, an unintersting hedge or some bare ground, or a large pergola or arbour to dress up, this may be what you are looking for. Specialists also recommend planting Kiftsgate near a pond or fountain to catch its reflection. However, you must let it grow without pruning it: it is naturally a wild flower and it should remain as one. It does not mind if it does not get a lot of sun.

Brenda Colvin, a daughter of Kiftsgate, is like her pretty mother but she is not quite so enormous. The flowers are bigger, semi-double and very fragrant, in a delightful pink that slowly fades to white.

Another rambler with abundant blossoms that can act in place of the other two is **Bobbie James**. This comes from a Japanese rose, the *wichuraiana*, also native to China and Formosa. It usually only grows to 30–35 feet (10 metres) and has a tremendously abundant bloom with creamy white flowers that are bigger and fuller.

Rosa filipes Kiftsgate

GOLDFINCH

Here we are in the realm of the small rambler, though it is only small relatively, ramblers by nature being robust and voluminous. But it is not quite in the same league as the *banksiae* or *Rosa filipes* Kiftsgate, whose vitality is enormous.

Within the limited definition of rambler belongs **Félicité et Perpétue**, a very old rose bearing the names of the two daughters of A A Jacques, the gardener of Louis Philippe of Orleans, later king of France. They will grow in gardens for more than 150 years and they last that long because they are of exceedingly good quality, descending from *Rosa sempervirens*. Under the right conditions they have small, shapely foliage all year round. The many branches, growing from the base, are thickly laden with small flowers, with many doubles among them, and thickly clustered, like pompons. The buds are red and open to a flesh-pink fading to delicate cream. The flowers also have a soft but intense scent that smells like primrose. A rambler that can be kept under control, but always ready to cover an arbour, it can grow up to 20 feet (6 metres). When pruning, cut it very little or not at all, trimming only those branches which have blossomed, shortly after they flower, or eliminating them completely.

If you do not have either a wall or an arbour, but you do not want to pass up this delightful rose, substitute **White Pet** for it, a smaller genetic mutation of Félicité et Perpétue.

Of even more modest dimensions and a descendant of *Rosa multiflora* is **Goldfinch**, which reaches only 10 feet (3 metres), so is also suitable for small gardens. I recommend it for its small, intensely scented flowers, with elegant buds and a changeable colour ranging from golden yellow and apricot-yellow to lemon-yellow; later the sun turns it milk and cream coloured. Goldfinch is good natured with shiny leaves, coppery anthers and almost thornless branches, and it reproduces easily from wood cuttings.

Another rose worth mentioning, also a hybrid of *Rosa multiflora*, crossed with a *moschata* this time, is **The Garland**, created in 1835. About 16 feet (5 metres) tall, with rather small, very strongly scented, semi-double flowers that are a creamy white suffused with pink, it flowers in June. What Miss Jekyll says of The Garland, and surely we can trust such a passionate rose-lover, is inviting. She advises getting up at four in the morning one day in the middle of June to go and have a look at the delicate charm of the buds as they are about to open. As charming as they are at midday, she says, they are even more charming waking up after the refreshing sleep of a brief

Goldfinch

summer night. In autumn there is a lovely mass of small red fruit.

A vigorous rambler with rather late flowers, coming from the Chinese *Rosa soulieana*, **Kew Rambler** bears the name of the famous botanical garden in London where it was born in 1912. It has delightful, small, pink flowers with a white centre and yellow stamens that grow in orderly clusters and are softly perfumed. They have a single flowering and produce orangeish fruit in autumn. Both their flowers and their orange fruit contrast nicely with their small, refined greyish leaves.

ROSES EVERYWHERE: PLANTING THEM TO BEST ADVANTAGE

Shade-tolerant Roses

Rosa farreri persetosa
Rosa x paulii
Rosa canina andersonii
Rosa roxburghii
Rosa bracteata
Rosa x anemonoides
Rosa chinensis mutabilis
Rosa chinensis Old Blush
Rosa brunoni La Mortola
Frühlingsgold
Frühlingsanfang
Frühlingsmorgen
Frühlingszauber
Frühlingsduft
Maiden's Blush
Königin von Dänemark
Félicité Parmentier
Celestial
Complicata
La Belle Sultane
Sissinghurst Castle
Kazanlik
Scarlachglut
Mary Queen of Scots
Duchesse de Montebello
Stanwell Perpetual
Mousseline
Mme Hardy
York and Lancaster
Mme Sancy de Parabère
Amy Robsart
Lord Penzance
Lady Penzance
Julia Mannering
Meg Merrilees
Green Mantle
Raubritter
Dortmund
Ballerina
Erfurt

Max Graf
Scabrosa
Rosa rugosa alba
Rosa x microrugosa
Frau Dagmar Hastrup
Blanc Double de Coubert
Belle Poitévine
Sarah van Fleet
Vanguard
Pink Grootendorst
Rosa filipes Kiftsgate
Brenda Colvin
Narrow Water
Bourbon Queen
Louise Odier
Mme Grégoire Staechelin
Cornelia
Eva
Felicia
Penelope
Francesca
Moonlight
Sadler's Wells
Iceberg
Mermaid
The Garland
Cocktail
Clair Matin
Bobbie James
Ghislaine de Féligonde
Goldfinch
Constance Spry
Soldier Boy
Sparrieshoop
Elmshorn
Yesterday
The Fairy
Escapade
New Dawn
Cupid

Roses for Poor Soil

Rosa x paulii
Rosa x cantabrigiensis
Rosa filipes Kiftsgate
Rosa richardii
Complicata
Frühlingsgold
Frühlingszauber
Frühlingsanfang
Frühlingsduft
Frühlingsmorgen
Amy Robsart
Lord Penzance
Lady Penzance
Julia Mannering
Meg Merrilees
Green Mantle
Golden Wings

Stanwell Perpetual
Leverkusen
Constance Spry
Rosa x alba suaveolens
Maiden's Blush
Königin von Dänemark
Félicité Parmentier
Bobbie James
Goldfinch
Ghislaine de Féligonde
Kew Rambler
Rosa x microrugosa
Blanc Double de Coubert
Scabrosa
Hansa
Frau Dagmar Hastrup
Max Graf

Roses to Plant in Groups

Mousseline
Celsiana
Kazanlik
Iceberg
Lilac Charm
Escapade
Dainty Maid
Pink Parfait
Belinda
Cornelia
Francesca

Felicia
Penelope
Eva
Vanity
Moonlight
Sadler's Wells
Tip Top
Apricot Nectar
Sarabande
Dapple Dawn
Rush

Roses for Large Hedges

Complicata
La Belle Sultane
Blanc Double de Coubert
Scabrosa
Frau Dagmar Hastrup
Rosa rugosa alba
Rosa x microrugosa
Pink Grootendorst
Celestial
Maiden's Blush
Königin von Dänemark
Rosa x alba semiplena
Frühlingsgold

Frühlingsanfang
Frühlingsmorgen
Frühlingsduft
Frühlingszauber
Amy Robsart
Lord Penzance
Lady Penzance
Julia Mannering
Meg Merrilees
Green Mantle
Celsiana
Nevada
Marguerite Hilling

Magenta
Golden Wings
Belle Amour
Bourbon Queen
Louise Odier
Heritage

Queen Elizabeth
Penelope
Eva
Cornelia
Moonlight

Roses for Small Hedges

Old Blush China
Rose des Meaux
Duchesse d'Angoulême
Duchesse de Montebello
Félicité Parmentier
George Vibert
Mousseline
Mousseux du Japon
Botzaris
Ispahan
Felicia
Francesca

Sadler's Wells
Ballerina
Erfurt
Iceberg
Wife of Bath
Red Coat
Nathalie Nypels
Yesterday
Dainty Maid
Radway Sunrise
Pink Parfait
White Pet

Roses as Barriers

Blanc Double de Coubert
Scabrosa
Frau Dagmar Hastrup
Rosa x microrugosa
Belle Poitévine
Agnes
Roseraie de l'Hay

Sarah van Fleet
Rosa sericea pteracantha
Constance Spry
Rosa x paulii
Rosa x cantabrigiensis
Mme Georges Bruant
Robusta

Creeping Roses
Ramblers

Rosa filipes Kiftsgate
The Garland
Blush Rambler
Tea Rambler
Bobbie James
Goldfinch
Ghislaine de Féligonde
Kew Rambler
Albertine

Albéric Barbier
American Pillar
Gerbe Rose
Rosa banksiae banksiae
Rosa banksiae lutea
Rosa banksiae lutescens
Félicité et Perpétue
Baltimore Belle

Climbers

Aimée Vibert
Rosa bracteata
Rosa chinensis mutabilis

Rosa brunoni La Mortola
Rosa x anemonoides
Altissimo

Aloha
Scharlachglut
Dortmund
Bantry Bay
Clair Matin
Cocktail
Constance Spry
Händel
Souvenir de la Malmaison
Céline Forestier
New Dawn
Coral Dawn

Mme Butterfly
Lady Sonia
Lady Waterlow
Mme Grégoire Staechelin
Soldier Boy
Ramona
Mermaid
Lucetta
Hero
Meg
Cupid
Silver Moon

Prostrate Roses (maximum height 3ft/90cm)

Max Graf
Rosa x paulii
Rosa richardii
Rosa bracteata
Nozomi
Red Blanket
Dunwich Rose
Snow Carpet
Smarty
Raubritter
The Fairy

Candy Rose
Ferdy
Fairyland
Swany
Rosy Cushion
Scintillation
Wild Flower
Sea Foam
Pink Wave
Comet
Bonica

Small Roses (maximum height 3ft/90cm) for Small Gardens, Rock Gardens and Terraces

Rose des Meaux
White Pet
Pretty Jessica
Wife of Bath
Comte de Chambord
George Vibert
Mousseline
St Nicholas
Yesterday

Dainty Maid
Gruss an Aachen
Warwick Castle
Prospero
Nathalie Nypels
Pink Parfait
Shot Silk
Fleurette
Belinda

Miniature Roses for Pots, Balconies and Borders

Tesorino
Pink Meillandina
Lady Meillandina
Striped Meillandina
Yellow Meillandina
White Meillandina

San Valentino
Serenella
Mirandolina
Baby Masquerade
Fairy Changeling
Little Jewel

Cold-tolerant Roses

Rosa pimpinellifolia — Princess of Nassau
Rosa pimpinellifolia hispida — Stanwell Perpetual
Rosa pimpinellifolia altaica — Robbie Burns
Rosa x harisonii — Thérèse Bugnet
Rosa brunoni — Paul's Himalayan Musk

Good cold resistance is offered generally by *rugosa* and *eglanteria* roses and their hybrids, and by hybrids of *pimpinellifolia*.

Roses with Few or No Thorns

Agatha
Belle de Crécy
Cardinal de Richelieu
Hippolyte
Empress Josephine
Sissinghurst Castle
Tuscany
Tuscany Superb
Fantin-Latour
Rosa californica plena
Reine des Violettes
Rosa banksiae
Rosa banksiae alba plena

Rosa banksiae lutea
Rosa banksiae lutescens
Ghislaine de Féligonde
Zéphirine Drouhin
Goldfinch
Paul's Scarlet
Pink Parfait
Yvonne Rabier
Fashion
Iceberg (*climbing*)
Bettina (*climbing*)
Félicité e Perpétue
Dupuy Jamain

Roses with Decorative Fruit

Rosa arvensis
Rosa canina andersonii
Rosa multiflora
Rosa helenae
Rosa longicuspis
Rosa davidii
Rosa caudata
Rosa farreri persetosa
Rosa macrophylla doncasteri
Rosa sericea Heather Muir
Rosa roxburghii
Rosa villosa
Rosa moyesii Geranium
Rosa moyesii highdownensis
Rosa filipes Kiftsgate
Rosa rugosa alba
Rosa x microrugosa
Blanc Double de Coubert

Frau Dagmar Hastrup
Vanguard
Hansa
Scabrosa
Max Graf
Mary Queen of Scots
Dunwich Rose
Celsiana
Amy Robsart
Lord Penzance
Lady Penzance
Meg Merrilees
St Nicholas
Scarlachglut
Mme Grégoire Staechelin
Fritz Nobis
Kew Rambler

Plants to Grow with Roses

Large shrubs

Ceanothus
Hydrangea paniculata
Kolkwitzia

Weigela
Cornus florida
Ribes

Climbers

Jasminum
Clematis

Lonicera

Bulbs

Narcissus
Chionodoxa
Muscari
Crocus

Allium
Galanthus
Scilla

Herbs and small shrubs

Alyssum
Fragaria vesca
Potentilla
Thymus
Nepeta mussinii
Origanum majorana
Salvia
Lavandula

Rosmarinus
Santolina
Artemisia
Phlox
Fuchsia
Paeonia
Viburnum x burkwoodii

USEFUL ADDRESSES

Specialists and Retail Nurseries in Great Britain, Europe and the United States

In most major garden centres one can find a variety of roses, especially the Modern rose. Below are some addresses that you may find useful in your search for species, Old roses and others.

Great Britain

David Austin Roses, Bowling Green Lane, Albrighton, Wolverhampton WV7 8EA, specialists in old roses

Peter Beales Roses, London Road, Attleborough, Norfolk NR17 1AY, specialists in old roses

R Harkness & Co Ltd, The Rose Garden, Hitchin, Herts SG4 0JT

LeGrice Roses, Norwich Road, North Walsham, Norfolk NR28 0DR

Hillier Nurseries (Winchester) Ltd, Ampfield House, Ampfield, Romsey, Hants SO5 9PA

Europe

Meilland, Boulevard Francis Meilland 134, Cap d'Antibes, 06601 France

W Kordes Sohne, Rosenschule, Rosenstrasse 54, 2206 Klein Offenseth-Sparrieshoop, Holstein, West Germany

Rosen Tantau, Postfach 1344, 2082 Uetersen bei Hamburg, West Germany

D T Poulsen Planteskole, ApS 60, Kelleriisveg, DK 3490 Kvistgaard, Denmark

United States

Armstrong Nurseries Inc, PO Box 4060, Ontario, CA 91761

Kelly Bros Nurseries Inc, 650 Maple Street, Dansville, NY 14437

Roses of Yesterday and Today, 802 Brown Valley Road, Watsonville, CA 95076

Wyant Roses Inc, Melvin E Wyant, Rose Specialist, 9259 Johany Cake Ridge, Mentor, OH 44060

For more information about roses and locating hard-to-find roses, write to the Rose Growers Association, 303 Mile End Road, Colchester, Essex CO4 5EA.

In the United States, write to the American Rose Society, PO Box 30,000, Shreveport, LA 71130, which is one of the largest and most active rose societies in America, with many publications.

BIBLIOGRAPHY

Austin, David *The Rose*, 1987
Beales, Peter *Classic Roses*, 1985
Gault, S Millar and Synge, P M *The Dictionary of Roses in Colour*, 1971
Gibson, Michael *The Book of the Rose*, 1980
    Growing Roses, 1984
Griffiths, Trevor *My World of Old Roses*, 1984
Harkness, Paul *Roses*, 1978
Jekyll, Gertrude and Mawley, E *Roses for English Gardens*, 1902
Kordes, Wilhelm *Rosen*, 1935
LeGrice, E B *Rose Growing Complete*, 1965
Thomas, G S *The Old Shrub Roses*, 1961
    Shrub Roses of Today, 1962
    Climbing Roses Old and New, 1978
Willmott, E A *The Genus Rosa*, 1910, 1914

INDEX

Numbers in italics indicate pages with illustrations.